To Catch a Thief

"My star is gone!" Winston yelled. He was standing next to the holiday spirit display. "Christmas won't be the same without my star."

"Oh, so now you're upset," Lila snapped. "When my pin was stolen, all you cared about was your lunch."

Jessica sighed. "Listen," she whispered to the other Snoopers. "Mrs. Otis always locks the door when we go to lunch. That means someone in this classroom must have taken Winston's star."

"Are you saying one of us is a thief?" Eva asked.

"Not one of us Snoopers," Todd said. "But Jessica is right. Someone in the class must be taking things."

The Snoopers all looked at each other.

"We have to catch the thief," Jessica said.

Bantam Skylark Books in the SWEET VALLEY KIDS series

SWEET VALLEY KIDS SUPER SNOOPER EDITIONS

SWEET VALLEY KIDS
SUPER SNOOPER #4

THE CASE
OF THE
CHRISTMAS
THIEF

Written by
Molly Mia Stewart

Created by
FRANCINE PASCAL

Illustrated by
Ying-Hwa Hu

A BANTAM SKYLARK BOOK®
NEW YORK • TORONTO • LONDON • SYDNEY • AUCKLAND

RL 2, 005–008

THE CASE OF THE CHRISTMAS THIEF
A Bantam Skylark Book / December 1992

*Sweet Valley High® and Sweet Valley Kids are trademarks of
Francine Pascal*

Conceived by Francine Pascal

*Produced by Daniel Weiss Associates, Inc.
33 West 17th Street
New York, NY 10011*

Cover art by Susan Tang

*Skylark Books is a registered trademark of Bantam Books, a division
of Bantam Doubleday Dell Publishing Group, Inc. Registered in U.S.
Patent and Trademark Office and elsewhere.*

ISBN 0-553-48063-4

Published simultaneously in the United States and Canada

*Bantam Books are published by Bantam Books, a division of Bantam
Doubleday Dell Publishing Group, Inc. Its trademark, consisting of the
words "Bantam Books" and the portrayal of a rooster, is Registered in
U.S. Patent and Trademark Office and in other countries. Marca Regis-
trada. Bantam Books, 666 Fifth Avenue, New York, New York 10103.*

PRINTED IN THE UNITED STATES OF AMERICA

OPM   0 9 8 7 6 5 4 3 2 1

To Barry Lawrence Sasson

CHAPTER 1

Holiday Spirit

"I can't wait to show everyone our cookie cutter," Jessica Wakefield whispered to her twin sister, Elizabeth. "I wish Mrs. Otis would hurry up and finish taking attendance."

Elizabeth smiled. "Me, too. I can't wait to see what everyone else brought in. The holiday show-and-tell was a great idea."

It was late December at Sweet Valley Elementary School. The twins' second-grade teacher, Mrs. Otis, had asked each student to bring in the object that made him or her feel the most holiday spirit. The twins had brought in their favorite Christmas cookie cutter.

Finally the teacher finished taking attendance. "OK, class," she said with a smile. "It's time to share your special holiday objects. Who would like to go first?"

Almost every hand in the class went up immediately. But Jessica's shot up fastest of all.

Mrs. Otis laughed. "I'm glad to see that you're all so anxious to spread your holiday spirit. Jessica, why don't you start?"

Jessica stood up. She grabbed Elizabeth's hand and pulled her up, too. "We brought in something together," she explained.

"That's no surprise," Kisho Murasaki called out.

"No surprise at all," Mrs. Otis agreed.

It was no surprise because Jessica and

Elizabeth were identical twins. They both had blue-green eyes and long blond hair with bangs. When they dressed alike, even their closest friends had trouble telling them apart.

Even though the twins looked alike on the outside, they were very different on the inside. Elizabeth loved school, reading books, and all kinds of sports. Jessica loved recess, talking to her friends, and playing with her dollhouse. The twins even had different favorite colors. Jessica's was pink, and Elizabeth's was green.

But even though they had many different interests, Jessica and Elizabeth were best friends. And one interest they had in common was solving mysteries. The twins and some of their friends had even started their own detective club called the Snoopers, and they were always looking for a new mystery to solve.

"This is a cookie cutter we use to make Christmas cookies," Jessica told the class. She held up the cookie cutter so that everyone could see it.

"See? It's shaped like Santa Claus," Elizabeth said. "After the cookies come out of the oven, our whole family helps to decorate them with frosting and sprinkles."

"That sounds like fun," Mrs. Otis said.

Jessica nodded. "Eating them is fun, too," she said with a smile.

Everyone laughed. "Thank you, girls," Mrs. Otis said. "OK, who's next?"

The twins' classmates raised their hands again. Winston Egbert waved his eagerly.

"OK, Winston, go ahead," Mrs. Otis said.

Winston stood up and carefully held up a delicate silver ornament. "This is the star my family puts on top of our Christmas tree every year. My mother's family had it when

she was a little girl. My grandfather bought it before my mother was even born."

"It's beautiful," Mrs. Otis said. "And I'm sure it's a nice feeling to use something that's been in your family for so long."

"It is," Winston said.

Lila Fowler went next. She showed the class a hand-painted reindeer pin. "My mother bought it for me in Norway," she explained. "She gave it to me for my very first Christmas present, when I was a baby. But I wasn't allowed to wear it until last year."

Then Mrs. Otis called on Todd Wilkins. Todd stood up and held out a pair of socks. Elizabeth, Jessica, and some of the other kids started to giggle.

"Don't laugh," Todd told them. "These are my very favorite socks. My grandmother knitted them for me. I only wear them on

Christmas Day. See, they're decorated with candy canes."

Andy Franklin stood up next. "My family's Jewish," he said. "We celebrate Hanukkah." He held up something that looked like a top, with Hebrew letters on four sides. "This is a dreidel," he said. "We use it to play a special Hanukkah game. It's really fun."

The other kids in the class showed off their holiday objects one by one. Amy Sutton had brought in the special plate her family used every year to leave out cookies for Santa. Eva Simpson showed everyone the book of Christmas stories her father read out loud every Christmas Eve. Julie Porter had brought a pair of china candlesticks decorated with holly. Ellen Riteman showed everyone the stocking she hung up on the night before Christmas.

Soon, only Ricky Capaldo had not shown

7

his holiday object. "Ricky, you've been very patient," Mrs. Otis said. "You're the last one to share what you brought."

"I didn't bring anything," Ricky said. "I forgot."

"That's too bad," Mrs. Otis said. "Try to remember tomorrow, and we'll make time to see it."

Ricky shrugged. "All right. But I don't care about Christmas."

Jessica looked at Elizabeth. "Ricky sure is grumpy," she whispered.

Elizabeth nodded. "Something must be bothering him. He's usually nice."

Before Jessica could answer, Mrs. Otis announced that it was time for everyone to put their objects on the display table she had set up for them. The day before, all the students had helped to make a sign that said "Our Holiday Spirit," and Mrs. Otis had hung it on the wall over a table covered with a pretty piece of holiday fabric. After Jessica had helped Elizabeth find a good place for their cookie cutter, she stepped back and grinned. The table looked beautiful. Jessica couldn't wait for Christmas.

CHAPTER 2

A Mysterious Disappearance

During morning recess, all anyone could talk about was the upcoming holiday. "What are you going to do over vacation?" Elizabeth asked Amy, Winston, and Ricky.

"My grandparents are coming to visit," Amy said. "I can't wait. They live in Texas. I haven't seen them since last summer."

"My cousins are coming from Los Angeles," Winston said. "Every Christmas Eve, we all go and play softball at Secca Lake. It's a family tradition."

Just then the bell rang, and they all headed inside.

"My baseball landed in Secca Lake at Kisho's birthday party," Ricky said. "I asked for a new one for Christmas."

"I want a pair of Rollerblades," Winston said.

"So do I," Elizabeth told Winston. "If we both get them, we can go skating together."

"Yeah, that would be cool," Winston said. He turned to Amy and Ricky. "You guys should ask for skates, too. Then you could come with us."

"I already have a pair of regular skates," Ricky said. "My mom got them for me last year. We used to go skating together all the time."

"Don't you go anymore?" Elizabeth asked.

Ricky shook his head. Elizabeth, Amy, Winston and Ricky walked into Mrs. Otis's classroom and stopped inside the door.

"Ricky's mom *can't* skate now," Winston told Elizabeth and Amy. "She's having a baby."

"Wow!" Amy said. "You never told us. Is the baby going to be born soon?"

"Around Christmas, I think," Ricky said with a shrug.

"Is it going to be a boy or a girl?" Elizabeth asked.

"I don't know," Ricky answered. "My parents say it doesn't matter. They'll be happy either way."

"Maybe it will be twins," Elizabeth said.

Ricky frowned. Elizabeth wanted to ask him what was wrong. But before she could say anything, she heard a loud scream. She turned and saw Lila standing beside the Holiday Spirit display, looking very upset.

"My pin is gone!" she yelled.

Elizabeth and the other second-graders gathered around Lila. Mrs. Otis hurried over, too. "Your pin can't be gone. I'm sure it's here somewhere," Mrs. Otis told Lila. "We'll find it."

But even though Lila and Mrs. Otis searched everywhere, Lila's pin was nowhere to be found.

"It's really gone," Lila said with a sob. "Christmas can *not* go on without my reindeer pin."

"Come on, Lila. Cheer up," Mrs. Otis said. "We'll find your pin."

"I doubt it," Lila said. "Someone stole it. It's gone forever."

"Now, Lila," Mrs. Otis said. "Where's your holiday spirit?"

"It's gone, too," Lila said. She stomped over to her desk and sat down.

Jessica poked her sister in the shoulder. "You know what we have to do now, don't you?" she whispered.

Elizabeth nodded. "Find Lila's pin. And

that means calling in some expert detectives."

"The Snoopers!" Jessica said.

"We'll meet during lunch," Elizabeth said. "Pass the word."

CHAPTER 3

The Thief Strikes Again

When it was time for lunch, the Snoopers—Elizabeth, Jessica, Lila, Amy, Todd, Winston, Eva, and Ellen—sat down together at a table in a corner of the cafeteria. They wanted to be able to discuss the mystery of Lila's missing pin in private.

"We've already looked everywhere," Lila said sadly. "I know someone stole it. Now I'll never get it back."

Elizabeth smiled at her. "Don't worry. The Snoopers are on the case."

Lila looked doubtful. "I don't know. I think this is a job for experts. I'm going to tell my father to call the police."

"I'll bet the police won't even look for it," Todd said. "It's not that valuable or anything."

Lila's eyes filled with tears. "It's valuable to me. It was my first Christmas present from my mother."

Elizabeth put her arm around Lila's shoulder. "We know. That's why the Snoopers are the only ones who can solve this case. We're the only ones who know how important your pin really is."

Lila sniffed and shrugged. "I guess. But I'm sure it's gone forever."

"Come on, you guys, lunch will be over soon," Amy said. "We've got to think."

Winston took a bite of his ham and cheese sandwich.

"Don't eat," Eva scolded him. "Think."

16

"Detectives need their strength," Winston mumbled. "Besides, I can eat and think at the same time."

"What are we trying to think of, anyway?" Ellen asked. "Lila's right. We already looked everywhere for her pin."

"I know," Elizabeth said. "That means that someone must have stolen it. We have to think of a plan to figure out who it was."

"Oh. I get it," Ellen said. "But how are we going to do that? We were all out at recess when it happened."

"I've got it," Todd exclaimed. "Visitors to the school have to sign in at the office. I'll go check to see if any visitors were here this morning." He jumped up and ran toward the principal's office.

"This could be our first clue," Eva said.

"I'm sure it must have been a visitor who took Lila's pin," Jessica said. "No one at

17

Sweet Valley Elementary would be mean enough to do something like that."

"I can't believe *anyone* would be mean enough to do something like that," Amy added.

"Me neither," Winston said, taking a big bite of a peanut-butter cookie.

"Winston, how can you eat at a time like this?" Lila demanded. "You're supposed to be finding my pin. You should act like a detective!"

"I can eat and detect at the same time," Winston muttered.

Elizabeth rolled her eyes at Jessica. At this rate the Snoopers weren't going to be able to solve anything.

Just then, Todd came running back from the office. "I checked the sign-in book," he told the Snoopers breathlessly. "There weren't any visitors in the building today."

Elizabeth and Jessica looked at each

18

other. "That means the thief is someone here at school," Elizabeth said.

Jessica nodded. "We've got to find out who."

"But how?" asked Eva.

"When we go back to class, let's ask everyone if they saw anyone from another class come into our room today," Amy suggested.

"Good idea," said Todd.

"Maybe a kindergartener took it," Eva said. "Someone that young might not know any better."

For the first time, Lila looked hopeful. "Eva's right. It must have been a kindergartener. Maybe I'll get my pin back after all."

"If a kindergartener came into our room, I'm sure someone would have noticed," Elizabeth said, looking excited. "So we'll do what Amy said, and ask everyone. This could be our easiest case yet."

A few minutes later the bell rang, and the Snoopers hurried back to class. They wanted to have plenty of time to question their classmates. Elizabeth walked up to Jerry McAllister. "Did you see anyone take Lila's pin?" she asked him.

"Nope," said Jerry.

"Did you notice anyone from another class hanging around our room this morning?" Elizabeth asked.

"What are you, the police?" Jerry asked with a snicker. "No, Detective Wakefield, I didn't see anyone suspicious." He walked away, laughing loudly.

Elizabeth shrugged and looked around for someone else to ask. She saw that Jessica was talking to Caroline Pearce. Elizabeth walked over.

"Jerry didn't see anything," Elizabeth told her sister.

"Caroline just told me she didn't, either," Jessica said.

"But if you find out who did it, make sure you tell me right away," Caroline said. She liked to know about everything that happened in Mrs. Otis's class.

"Come on, let's go talk to Sandy Ferris," Elizabeth said after Caroline had walked away.

Jessica nodded. But before the twins could take a step, they heard an angry shout. It was Winston. "My star is gone!" he yelled. He was standing next to the Holiday Spirit display. "I can't believe it."

Mrs. Otis hurried over to help Winston search for his star. She looked worried. "Don't panic, everyone. Let's all help Winston look. His ornament must be here somewhere."

21

But even though everyone helped search the whole room, Winston's star was nowhere to be found.

"Christmas won't be the same without my star," Winston moaned.

"Oh, so now you're upset," Lila snapped. "When my pin was stolen, all you cared about was your lunch."

"Shut up, Lila," Winston shouted. "My star is important to my whole family. We can't have Christmas without it. All you lost was a stupid piece of jewelry."

"All right, Lila, Winston, that's enough," Mrs. Otis said sternly. "We're never going to solve anything by yelling. Take your seats."

Lila and Winston stomped off to their seats.

"Listen," Jessica whispered to the other Snoopers as they walked back toward their desks. "Mrs. Otis always locks the door

when we go to lunch. That means someone in this classroom must have taken Winston's star."

"Are you saying one of us is a thief?" Eva asked, wide-eyed.

Todd nodded. "I'm sure it's not one of us Snoopers," he said. "But someone in the class is taking things."

The Snoopers all looked at each other.

"We have to catch the thief," Jessica said.

CHAPTER 4

A Big Decision

Jessica looked up from her spelling list as Mrs. Armstrong, the principal, walked into the room. Mrs. Armstrong spoke quietly with Mrs. Otis for a few minutes. Then she turned and faced the students. "Mrs. Otis asked me to come by because it seems some things have disappeared from this classroom," the principal said. "I like to think that we all respect each other enough not to take what isn't ours."

Jessica glanced around at her class-mates. She was hoping somebody would look guilty, but nobody did.

"I'm sure all of you know stealing is wrong," Mrs. Armstrong went on. "But the important thing is not to punish the person who took Lila's and Winston's belongings. The important thing is to have their objects returned in time for Christmas."

"Thank you, Mrs. Armstrong," Mrs. Otis said as the principal finished. After Mrs. Armstrong had closed the classroom door behind her, Mrs. Otis turned to the class. "I know everyone here is unhappy that Lila's pin and Winston's star are missing," she said. "Now, I'm going to ask you all to close your eyes. I want you all to promise not to peek. I'll close my eyes, too. Whoever took Lila's pin and Winston's star can leave them on my desk. No questions asked. OK?"

Everyone nodded.

"Good. Now, close your eyes," Mrs. Otis instructed. "And keep them closed. I'm closing mine now, too. No peeking."

The room grew quiet. It was so quiet that Jessica could hear the clock on the wall ticking. She was so curious that she didn't know if she could keep herself from peeking. She wanted to know if someone was putting the missing things on Mrs. Otis's desk. But she kept her eyes squeezed shut.

The seconds seemed to go by very slowly. Jessica wondered how long Mrs. Otis would make them wait.

"You can open your eyes now," the teacher said finally.

Jessica opened her eyes and looked at Mrs. Otis's desk. There was nothing there. She heard Lila and Winston groan.

"I'm very disappointed," Mrs. Otis said. "And because Winston's and Lila's Christmas objects have not been returned, the rest of you may keep your things with you for the rest of the day and take them home tonight. Go ahead and get them now."

Jessica felt a tug on her sleeve as she got up. It was Elizabeth. "What is it?" Jessica asked.

"Wait," Elizabeth whispered. "Get the rest of the Snoopers."

Jessica and Elizabeth called out to Amy, Ellen, Todd, and Eva.

"We have to leave our things here," Elizabeth whispered to them when they all were gathered around her. "It's the only way we can solve the mystery."

Ellen's mouth dropped open. "What are you talking about? I'm not leaving my

28

stocking. It might get stolen." The others nodded.

"If everyone takes their stuff home," Elizabeth whispered, "how are we going to catch the thief?"

Todd shrugged. "I don't know, but I don't want anyone taking my socks."

"What if our things disappear?" Eva said, looking worried.

"And what if we don't solve the case?" Ellen asked. "Everything could get stolen and we'd never see it again."

"Stop acting like little kids," Elizabeth said firmly. "We have a mystery to solve. And we're not going to solve it by thinking we can't. Besides, we Snoopers should stick together. We have to help Lila and Winston get their stuff back."

Jessica took Elizabeth's hand. "Liz is right. We have to catch the thief. And the

only way we're going to be able to do it is by leaving our things here."

"Well, I don't want to," Ellen grumbled.

"Kids," Mrs. Otis called to them. "Are you going to come get your objects?"

"No, thanks," Jessica said quickly. "Liz and I are leaving our cookie cutter there."

Elizabeth smiled at her sister and looked at the other Snoopers. She hoped they would say the same thing.

"What about the rest of you?" the teacher asked.

"My book . . ." Eva paused and glanced at the twins anxiously. "Stays."

"My plate, too," Amy added.

"And I'm leaving my socks," Todd said softly.

There was a long pause. Elizabeth poked Ellen.

"I guess I'll leave my stocking, too," Ellen finally said.

"Thanks," Elizabeth told her fellow Snoopers as they walked back to their desks. "Leaving our stuff here will be worth it. It's the only way to solve the mystery."

CHAPTER 5

The First Clue

The next day at morning recess, all the Snoopers could talk about was the missing holiday objects. Lila and Winston hadn't stopped complaining about their things all day.

"It's not fair. My pin got stolen, and all of your stuff is still there," Lila said grumpily. "My whole Christmas is ruined."

"Mine's ruined, too," Winston said. "I still can't believe someone stole my star."

"Aren't you two ever going to cheer up?" Eva asked.

"No," Lila said. "It's stupid to be cheerful when there's a dangerous thief around."

Todd laughed. "Dangerous? Come on. You can't stay upset about this forever."

"Oh, yeah?" said Winston. "That's easy for you to say."

"Ricky's lucky he forgot to bring in his holiday object yesterday. I wish I had," Lila added with a frown.

Nothing the others said made Lila or Winston cheer up. After recess, Jessica and Elizabeth went inside together and sat down at their desks. "We've got to find the thief," Jessica said. "If we don't, Lila and Winston are going to drive us all crazy."

Elizabeth nodded. "I wonder why nothing else has disappeared?"

34

"I bet the thief is scared to take anything now," Jessica said.

"Do you think he knows we're watching?" Elizabeth asked.

But before Jessica could answer, the twins heard a yell from the Holiday Spirit table.

"My socks are gone," Todd cried.

Everyone rushed over to the table. "Now, don't worry, everyone," Mrs. Otis said as she hurried over. But Jessica thought that the teacher looked pretty worried herself.

"My socks have disappeared," Todd whimpered. "The thief has them. What am I going to tell my grandmother?"

"Calm down, Todd," Mrs. Otis said. "Getting upset won't help."

Todd stomped his foot. "I don't care."

"Well, it was pretty dumb to leave your socks here after my pin was stolen," Lila said.

"Shut up about your stupid pin," Todd said angrily. "We have to find my socks."

"Please, everyone, try to think," Mrs. Otis said. "Now, Todd, when was the last time you saw your socks?"

"They were here before recess," Todd said.

Ellen pushed Todd aside and grabbed her stocking off the table. "I'm taking this home before it's too late."

Mrs. Otis sighed. "That's not a bad idea, Ellen." The teacher turned to Amy, Eva, and the twins. "I think the rest of you had better keep your things in your desks for the rest of the day, too. Obviously someone is determined to spoil Christmas for everyone. I just hope that person will return everything before vacation."

Amy, Eva, and the twins all looked at each other and shook their heads. "Mrs. Otis, we still want to leave our things here," Elizabeth spoke up. The others nodded.

Mrs. Otis looked concerned. "I don't know . . ." she began.

Todd pulled on the teacher's arm. "I thought we were looking for my socks."

Mrs. Otis turned back to Todd. Quickly, Jessica pulled Elizabeth, Amy, Eva, and Ellen aside. "Let's look for clues."

Ellen, Amy, and Eva began to examine the table. Elizabeth and Jessica started to question people.

"Lois," Jessica asked. "Did you see anybody come near the Holiday Spirit table?" Lois Waller sat near the display.

"No. I didn't notice anybody here all morning," Lois said.

"That can't be," Elizabeth reasoned. "Something is missing. Somebody must have been here."

"Maybe a ghost took Todd's socks," Lois suggested.

Jim Sturbridge had heard the twins' question. He leaned forward from his seat behind Lois. "Lois, you must be blind if you didn't see anybody. Ken and Charlie and Julie and Ricky and Caroline and Jerry and Sandy and Andy and Kisho and Suzie all came by the Holiday Spirit display this morning."

Jessica and Elizabeth looked at Lois.

"I—I didn't see them," Lois stammered.

Jessica looked suspicious. "That's impossible."

"Are you positive you didn't see anyone?" Elizabeth said.

Lois's face was bright red. "Stop looking at me that way! I'm not the thief. My mom always says I daydream too much. I guess I just wasn't paying attention."

"I believe you, Lois," Elizabeth said.

Jessica nodded. She knew Lois could be forgetful sometimes. "This case isn't going anywhere," she said to Elizabeth as they walked away.

Elizabeth turned to look at Lila, Winston, and Todd. They were arguing with each other. "It sure would go faster if *all* of the Snoopers helped," she said.

"I know," Jessica agreed. "I'm going to write down the names of the people Jim saw at the display." But she still felt worried. She was afraid that her cookie cutter would be the next thing to disappear.

Just then Ellen ran up. "We found something," she exclaimed.

Elizabeth and Jessica followed Ellen back to the table. Ellen showed the twins a pair of footprints. They weren't prints of a whole shoe, though—only the tip of a shoe. The most interesting thing was that the

prints were blue. Whoever had made them must have spilled blue paint on his or her shoes.

Jessica grinned. "This is a real clue. Now we're getting somewhere."

CHAPTER 6

A Likely Suspect

Mrs. Otis helped Todd look for his socks for a few more minutes. Then she walked to the front of the class. Elizabeth could see that the teacher was frowning.

"OK, kids, let's settle down," Mrs. Otis said, clapping her hands. "It's time to work on our holiday art projects."

The class was making Christmas and Hanukkah presents for their friends and families. Everyone helped get out the supplies, and soon construction paper, paint, and sparkles covered the art tables. There were big pots of paste everywhere.

All the Snoopers were sitting together at one table. "I hope my parents like the Christmas-tree ornament I'm making them," Eva said.

"What is it?" asked Amy.

"It's a picture of my family sitting together on Christmas Eve while my father reads to us from our special book," Eva explained. She held up the ornament so the others could see. Then she got up from the table. "I'm going to go look at the book so I can copy it." She headed toward the Holiday Spirit display.

"I can't wait to give Mom our present," Elizabeth said. She and Jessica were making their mother an ornament shaped like the Wakefields' house.

43

"I can't wait for Christmas," Jessica replied happily.

Lila frowned. "Don't say that word in front of me."

"Lila's right. I wish you guys would stop acting so happy," Todd said. "Christmas won't be the same for some of us, you know."

Winston nodded. But before he could start complaining, too, there was a loud scream from Eva. "My book! It's gone!" she cried.

The rest of the Snoopers jumped up and ran over to the display. Elizabeth felt terrible. She had convinced Todd and Eva to leave their things at school, and now Todd's socks and Eva's book were missing.

"What are we going to do?" Eva asked Elizabeth. "Christmas can't go on without my book."

"Eva, you were looking forward to Christ-

44

mas just a few minutes ago," Elizabeth said. "Losing your book isn't going to change that. It's not a big deal."

"Elizabeth, be quiet," Eva said, starting to cry.

"Yeah," Todd added. "Leave Eva alone."

"Eva can be unhappy if she wants to," Lila snapped.

"Don't yell at Elizabeth," Jessica told Lila and Todd angrily. "She was just trying to make Eva feel better."

Mrs. Otis came over and gave Eva a hug. Then she walked back up to the front of the room. "Everyone sit down, please," she said sternly. Elizabeth could tell the teacher was running out of patience.

As the classroom grew quiet, Mrs. Otis said, "Someone here has disappointed me deeply. You know who you are."

Mrs. Otis looked out over the room. Elizabeth couldn't tell who the teacher was looking at.

"I don't know why you would want to hurt your friends," Mrs. Otis went on. "I only ask that you come forward before vacation begins and return the missing items. OK, everybody, get back to work on your presents."

"I'm sure glad I took my special wreath home," Caroline said loudly as she headed back to one of the art tables. "I never would have guessed I was going to school with a thief."

Elizabeth hoped that the thief would do as Mrs. Otis asked and come forward. But in case that didn't happen, she knew it was up to the Snoopers to find the missing objects. "Come on," she told Jessica, Ellen, and Amy. "Let's look for more clues."

"OK," Jessica said. "But where? We've looked everywhere."

"I know," Ellen said. She pointed at the display table. "We haven't looked under the table. Somebody crawl under there and look."

"Why don't *you* crawl under and look?" Amy asked.

"I don't want to get my clothes dirty," Ellen answered. "The table is a mess."

Elizabeth looked and saw that globs of something white were smeared all over the Holiday Spirit table.

Amy leaned forward. "What is this?"

"It's paste," Elizabeth said, touching one of the white globs with her finger.

Amy leaned even closer. "It's a paste handprint."

"Quick, get the other Snoopers," Elizabeth said, sounding excited. "This is an important clue."

Jessica ran over to the art table and got Lila, Todd, Winston, and Eva.

47

"What is it now?" Lila asked as she stomped over.

"Look," Amy said, pointing at the paste handprint.

"Big deal," Lila said with a shrug.

"So, it's paste," Todd added grumpily. "What does that prove?"

"It proves that the thief is someone messy," Amy said.

"Don't forget the footprints," Elizabeth reminded them. "The thief is someone messy who likes the color blue."

Jessica's eyes widened. "I know! I'll bet it's Charlie Cashman," she said.

Charlie Cashman often acted like a bully. He loved to tease people. And he was very messy.

Lila gasped. "You're probably right, Jessica. Charlie is the only one mean enough to take my pin. He'd better not break it!"

Elizabeth knew they didn't have enough

clues to tell for sure, but she had to agree that Charlie seemed like the most likely suspect. "We'd better be sure before we say anything," she said. "Let's watch him."

"All right," Ellen said. "Everyone watch Charlie!"

Amy turned to look in Charlie's direction. "He doesn't have blue stains on either of his shoes," she pointed out.

"He could have wiped the paint off," Jessica said.

"Look at his hands," Amy whispered. Charlie was teasing Suzie Nichols, pretending he was going to rub his hands in her hair.

"His hands are covered with paste," Ellen exclaimed.

"It has to be him," Todd said. "Let's get him!" He started toward Charlie, with the others right behind him.

"Wait," Elizabeth said. "We don't know for sure—"

But Todd didn't pay attention to her. "Charlie Cashman, give me my socks now," he yelled.

Charlie stopped chasing Suzie and turned to face Todd. He looked surprised. "Your what?"

"My Christmas socks," Todd said.

"Why would I want your smelly old socks?" Charlie asked.

"How about my pin?" Lila asked. "You didn't break it, did you?"

"Your pin?" Charlie started to laugh, but then his face turned red. "You guys think I'm the thief, don't you?"

"Don't act so innocent," Winston said.

"I *am* innocent," Charlie said. He marched over to his cubbie. "Go ahead and look if you don't believe me. Your stuff isn't in there."

Elizabeth stepped forward and peered inside Charlie's cubbie. She saw a squashed peanut-butter-and-jelly sandwich, a bunch of old spelling tests, and some action figures. "Nothing here," she said, straightening up.

"Maybe he took the stuff home," Lila said. She still looked suspicious.

"He couldn't have taken Eva's book home," Jessica pointed out. "It just disappeared."

"Sorry," Amy told Charlie.

Charlie shrugged and walked away without another word. He still looked angry. Elizabeth didn't blame him. She knew they shouldn't have accused him of being the thief without definite proof.

"OK, so it's not Charlie," Todd mumbled.

"It's not Charlie," Elizabeth agreed. "But we're getting closer. Every time the thief takes something, we get another clue."

"But almost everything is gone," Amy pointed out.

Elizabeth turned to look at the table. Only the twins' cookie cutter and Amy's cookie plate were still on it. Elizabeth bit her lip. The Snoopers were running out of time.

CHAPTER 7

The Secret Spies

After art class, Mrs. Otis went to the board and started writing math problems. Jessica looked around the room. Elizabeth was staring down at her desk, looking thoughtful. Jessica knew that her sister must be thinking about the thefts. Amy kept glancing back at the Holiday Spirit table to make sure her plate was still there. Winston had his head in both hands. He looked sad.

Jessica sighed. She knew that the

Snoopers didn't have much time to solve the mystery. Today was the last day of school before winter break.

Then she had an idea. Yesterday the thief had taken Winston's star during lunch. Maybe he or she would try to take something during lunch today, too. Nobody was allowed to stay in the classroom during lunch period, but if some of the Snoopers could do it anyway, they might be able to catch the thief. And Jessica had the perfect plan. She quickly wrote a note and passed it to her twin.

Elizabeth read the note, then turned to Jessica and nodded. Elizabeth passed the note to Amy.

Amy read the note. She gave the twins a thumbs-up sign. Then Amy passed the note back to the twins so they could give it to Ellen. After Ellen read it she nodded, too.

When the bell rang for lunch, Jessica,

Elizabeth, and Ellen stood in front of the coat closet. Because it was warm in Sweet Valley for most of the year, the closet was usually empty.

"Line up, everyone," Mrs. Otis said.

Jessica, Elizabeth, and Ellen pretended to look for something on the floor of the closet. Amy was in line, watching Jessica.

When Jessica nodded at Amy, she turned and pointed toward the hallway. "Hey!" Amy shouted. "Look at that!"

Mrs. Otis and the others looked where Amy was pointing. Meanwhile, Jessica, Elizabeth, and Ellen slipped into the closet and closed the door behind them. It was dark inside, and the air was dusty. Jessica was afraid she might sneeze.

"What is it?" Jessica heard Mrs. Otis ask Amy. "I don't see anything."

"I thought I saw a reindeer," Amy answered.

"A reindeer?" Mrs. Otis said. "I think a little something to eat will do us all a lot of good." The door clicked shut.

Jessica, Elizabeth, and Ellen stood extra still until they were sure everyone had left the room. "Now all we have to do is wait for the thief to come in," Jessica whispered.

The three girls waited silently for what seemed like a very long time. "This is stupid," Ellen whispered after a while. "Besides, I'm hungry."

Just then Elizabeth caught her breath. "Shh! What was that?"

"What was what?" Jessica asked.

"That!" Elizabeth whispered.

Ellen gasped. "It sounds like footsteps out in the hall. The thief must be coming!"

Jessica's heart started beating fast. She heard the door to the classroom open. "What do we do now?" she asked in a hushed voice.

"Open the closet a tiny bit," Elizabeth whispered. "We have to see who it is."

Ellen didn't move. "Not me."

"I'll do it," Jessica said, stepping toward the door.

"Ouch!" Ellen yelled. "That was my foot!"

"Shhh!"

The footsteps were coming closer. Suddenly the closet door swung open.

"What are you girls doing in here? You're supposed to be eating lunch." It was Mrs. Otis. She looked very surprised.

The girls stepped out of the closet. "We were trying to catch the thief," Elizabeth admitted.

Mrs. Otis frowned. Then she patted Elizabeth on the shoulder. "Thanks for trying to help, but you know it's against the rules to stay in the room during lunch," she said. "Let me handle catching the thief, OK?

58

Now, hurry down to the lunchroom and eat."

Jessica, Elizabeth, and Ellen headed down the hall. When Ellen pushed open the big door that led into the lunchroom, Jessica could see Winston, Eva, Lila, and Todd sitting together at a table in the corner. "They look so sad," Jessica said, pointing to their friends.

Ellen nodded. "They're not even talking to each other."

"We have to solve the mystery," Jessica said. "We have to give them their holiday spirit back."

CHAPTER 8

The Empty Table

As soon as she entered the room after lunch, Elizabeth looked over toward the Holiday Spirit display. She gasped. "Oh, no! Look!" she cried, pointing. The thief had struck again. The table was completely empty.

Elizabeth, Jessica, and Amy rushed over to the table. Elizabeth couldn't believe her eyes. "The thief took our cookie cutter!"

"Forget about your cookie cutter," Amy said. "My plate is gone. How can I leave cookies for Santa without my special plate?"

Mrs. Otis hurried up to them. "Now, calm down, all of you. I know you're upset. But shouting and arguing won't bring your things back any faster. Take your seats, please, and get ready to finish your art projects."

Amy stamped her foot. "But I want my plate back. You have to find it now!"

"What about our cookie cutter?" Jessica asked.

Mrs. Otis gave them each a stern look. "I said, please take your seats now. We have a lot to do before the big party this afternoon. Ricky's mom, Todd's dad, and Caroline's mom will be here soon. We have to finish making our presents, wrap them up, and clean the room before they arrive."

Elizabeth, Jessica, and Amy stomped over to their seats. "We're never going to be able to solve the mystery now," Jessica said sadly. "Christmas is ruined."

Elizabeth couldn't help agreeing with her sister. Making Santa cookies with their special cookie cutter had always been one of her favorite things. She couldn't imagine Christmas without it.

As she was thinking about Christmas, Elizabeth remembered how her family always sang Christmas carols while the Santa cookies were baking. Without realizing what she was doing, Elizabeth quietly began to hum "Rudolph, the Red-Nosed Reindeer."

A few seconds later, Jessica began to hum along with her sister. Then Charlie, who sat in front of Elizabeth, started to sing. Caroline, Kisho, and Suzie joined in.

Before long, the entire class was singing along. Mrs. Otis was singing, too. And Elizabeth noticed that everyone was smiling.

After the first song had ended, Kisho started "Jingle Bells."

"I guess maybe Christmas isn't ruined after all," Elizabeth said to her sister with a smile as the rest of the class continued to sing.

Jessica nodded. "Even if we don't have our cookie cutter, we can still have fun."

Amy heard her. "You're right, Jessica. Christmas will be great even without my special plate."

Elizabeth frowned. "One thing still bothers me, though. The Snoopers couldn't solve the mystery."

"What do you mean, we couldn't?" Amy said with a grin. "The day isn't over."

Jessica nodded. "If we can get all the Snoopers to stop being upset and get to work, we might still crack this case before vacation starts!"

CHAPTER 9

Christmas Blues

During afternoon recess, the Snoopers gathered near the swings.

"OK, everybody," Jessica said. "We have an hour and a half before vacation. Let's go over our clues."

"We know the thief goes to Sweet Valley Elementary," Todd said.

"And he or she is in our class," Eva added.

"The thief likes blue," Amy said.

"He's messy," Winston added.

Jessica grinned. She was glad that all of the Snoopers were working together again. Then Jessica noticed Ricky sitting all alone on a bench nearby, looking unhappy.

Jessica remembered that Ricky had looked sad the day they had brought their Holiday Spirit things to school. In fact, Jessica couldn't remember the last time Ricky *hadn't* looked sad.

"I'm going to go try to cheer up Ricky," Jessica told the Snoopers. She walked over to him. "Merry Christmas!"

The rest of the Snoopers came over, too. "Merry Christmas!" they all said.

Ricky frowned. "How come you guys are so happy? All of your favorite things are gone."

"It's still Christmastime," Eva pointed out. "And even without my book, it's still my favorite holiday." The other Snoopers nodded.

"Well, I'm not going to celebrate Christmas this year," Ricky told them.

"Really?" Lila asked. "How come?"

Ricky shrugged.

Elizabeth looked thoughtful. "Does it have something to do with the new baby?"

Ricky frowned even harder. "Yes!" he said. "My mom talks about the baby all the time."

"She's probably just excited," Ellen said.

"She *is* excited," Ricky said. "My dad's excited, too. The baby is the only thing they ever talk about. They don't care about *me* anymore."

Elizabeth and Jessica exchanged surprised looks. Jessica could imagine how she would feel if she thought her parents didn't love her anymore. She could understand now why Ricky didn't feel like celebrating Christmas.

CHAPTER 10

Big Brother Andy

"Why do you think your parents don't love you anymore?" Elizabeth asked.

"My mom and dad are spending all of their time getting ready for the baby," Ricky said. "They bought a crib, a stroller, pink and blue curtains, and wallpaper with little teddy bears on it."

Winston stuck out his tongue. "Wallpaper with teddy bears? Gross!"

"That's not all," Ricky said. But then he stopped and his face turned red. "Forget it."

"Come on, Ricky," Amy said. "Tell us."

"Well," Ricky said. "I searched all the closets at home. I looked in the basement and the attic. But I didn't find even one Christmas present for me. I just found baby stuff. They forgot about me already." Ricky looked as though he was about to cry.

"I have an idea," Winston said. "Let's talk to Andy. His mom had a baby last month. I'll go get him." He ran off, and returned a minute later with Andy.

"Hi, you guys. What's up?" Andy said.

"We want to know about your baby sister," Eva said. "Do you like her?"

"Sure," Andy said. He looked proud. "Her name's Sara. She'll be a month old tomorrow. She can't do much yet. But I'm going to teach her how to count as soon as she can talk."

"Have your mom and dad been acting weird since Sara was born?" Todd asked.

Andy made a face. "They're tired a lot, but that's because Sara wakes up in the middle of the night and wants to be fed," Andy answered. "You know what? Sometimes my parents let *me* feed her. Mom says being a big brother is a very important job."

"Do your parents still do things with you?" Ricky asked. "Like going skating and stuff?"

Andy nodded. "Once a week, Mom or Dad does something with just me. Last week, Dad took me to the museum. And we do lots of stuff with Sara, too. We took her to the beach for the first time yesterday. It's fun not being the only kid in the family anymore."

"Psst," Elizabeth whispered to Jessica.

"Do you still have the names of the people Jim saw near the Holiday Spirit table?"

Jessica reached into her pocket. She pulled out a piece of paper and handed it to Elizabeth. "Here it is. Why do you want it?"

Elizabeth was already reading the list. "I'll tell you later."

CHAPTER 11

More Blue Paint

After recess, everyone hurried inside to finish their art projects. The Snoopers all sat down together at one of the art tables.

"Ricky, sit with us," Jessica said.

"OK." Ricky sat down next to Winston.

"What are you making?" Jessica asked him.

"A present for my mom," Ricky said. "Every Christmas, I make her an ornament to hang on the Christmas tree. See?" He held

it up. He had washed out a small milk carton and cut off the top. Then he had pasted a picture of Santa Claus inside. The outside of the carton was covered in blue construction paper. The ornament was messy, but pretty.

Mrs. Otis came over. She looked at Ricky's ornament and then carefully put it inside a bag he had colored blue. "That's a beautiful present, Ricky," Mrs. Otis said. She folded the top of the blue bag and stapled it shut. "There. Now all you need to do is tape a bow to the bag and it will be all ready."

"Great," Ricky said. He grabbed a big blue bow from the pile of ribbons and bows in the middle of the table.

"You made the ornament blue, you colored the bag blue, and you're putting a blue bow on it," Elizabeth said to Ricky. "Is blue your favorite color?"

"Yes," Ricky said. He waited until Mrs. Otis had walked away. "I'm not sure I'm going to give this to my mom, though," he said.

"Why not?" Amy asked.

"Because she keeps saying the baby is the best Christmas present in the whole world," Ricky said. "She probably doesn't even want a present from me."

Eva frowned. "Don't be silly."

"Yeah," Winston said. "Everyone *always* wants more presents. I know I do."

Ricky laughed.

"Maybe you should make a Christmas present for the baby, too," Elizabeth suggested.

"I don't know," Ricky said. "What would I make?"

"How about a picture of your family?" Eva suggested.

"That's a good idea," Jessica said. "You

could draw yourself, your parents, and your little brother or sister."

"You can hang it on the wall in the baby's room," Amy said.

Ricky smiled and began to draw. He used lots of blue paint. He put globs of paste down and covered everything with yellow sparkles.

Lila looked at the clock. "It's almost time for vacation!"

Jessica grinned. "Soon Liz and Mom and Dad and Steven and I will be making Christmas cookies—" Jessica lost her smile. "Without our special cookie cutter," she finished.

"Do you know what's really terrible?" Todd asked.

"We still didn't solve the case," Eva said.

"We're not very good detectives after all," Jessica said.

But Jessica noticed that Elizabeth was smiling. "Do you know something we don't?" she asked her sister.

"Maybe," Elizabeth answered mysteriously.

CHAPTER 12

Case Solved

"I hope everyone is finished," Mrs. Otis said. "Because it's time to clean up."

Everyone helped put away the crayons, paints, paste, construction paper, and sparkles. Mrs. Otis swept the floor. They had just finished cleaning when Mrs. Capaldo, Mrs. Pearce, and Mr. Wilkins arrived.

The party began right away. Mrs. Pearce put on a tape of holiday songs that she had brought. Mr. Wilkins passed out chocolate cupcakes and glasses of juice. And Mrs.

Capaldo gave each student a pencil decorated like a candy cane. Ricky helped her pass them out.

"Would you do me a big favor?" Mrs. Capaldo asked Ricky, after the last pencil had been given away. She pulled a shiny package out of her pocket. "Would you open this, please?"

"Is it for me?" Ricky seemed surprised.

"Of course," Mrs. Capaldo said. "Who else?"

Ricky took the present and ripped off the wrapping. When he lifted the lid of the box and saw what was inside, a big smile spread across Ricky's face. He held up a baseball for everyone to see.

"I didn't want to make you wait until Christmas," Mrs. Capaldo said. "Especially since your old baseball is at the bottom of Secca Lake."

"I thought you'd forgotten about me," Ricky said.

"Forgotten about you?" Mrs. Capaldo asked. "How could I ever do that? You're my favorite skating partner."

Ricky smiled. "I have a present for you, too," he told his mother. He handed her one of his blue bags.

Mrs. Capaldo opened it. "Oooh! This is beautiful," she said, pulling out the Santa Claus ornament and examining it from all sides. "In fact, it's the best ornament you've ever made." Mrs. Capaldo gave Ricky a hug. "I love it. And I love you, too."

"I made something else," Ricky said. He held up his other blue bag. "But you can't open this one because it's not for you."

"Is it for Daddy?" Mrs. Capaldo asked.

"Nope," Ricky said.

Mrs. Capaldo looked puzzled. "Who is it for?"

"It's for the baby," Ricky said.

"Ricky, that's wonderful," Mrs. Capaldo said. She looked very happy.

Ricky grinned.

"Maybe we didn't solve the case," Jessica whispered to Elizabeth. "But at least Ricky has his holiday spirit back. Hey! Wait a minute . . ." Jessica looked at the paste sticking to Ricky's fingers, and the big spots of blue paint on his shoes.

Elizabeth smiled. She knew Jessica had figured out who the thief was. "We just need one thing to solve the case," she announced to the other Snoopers. "Ricky's help."

Winston looked puzzled. "What do you mean?"

"Does Ricky know who took our stuff?" Ellen asked.

Without a word, Ricky went to his cubbie. He took out his book bag and unzipped it.

The Snoopers gathered around. Ricky reached into the bag and pulled out the twins' cookie cutter. Then he brought out Lila's pin, Winston's star, and all of the other Snoopers' things.

"I'm sorry," Ricky said, his face turning red. "I didn't think I'd have a good Christmas. I didn't want anyone else to have fun, either. I guess that wasn't very nice."

"No, it wasn't," Mrs. Otis said as she came over. "But I'm glad you're giving everything back."

Lila grinned as she pinned her reindeer pin to her shirt. "We solved the mystery."

Elizabeth took the cookie cutter from Ricky. She was glad to have it back. But

somehow it didn't seem as important as it had before.

"Holiday spirit can't really come from things, can it?" Jessica said.

"No way," Elizabeth said. "It only comes from people."

SWEET VALLEY KIDS

Jessica and Elizabeth have had lots of adventures in *Sweet Valley High* and *Sweet Valley Twins*...now read about the twins at age seven! You'll love all the fun that comes with being seven—birthday parties, playing dress-up, class projects, putting on puppet shows and plays, losing a tooth, setting up lemonade stands, caring for animals and much more! It's all part of SWEET VALLEY KIDS. Read them all!

Buy them at your local bookstore or use this handy page for ordering:

Bantam Books, Dept. SVT3, 2451 S. Wolf Road, Des Plaines, IL 60018

Please send me the items I have checked above. I am enclosing $_____
(please add $2.50 to cover postage and handling). Send check or money
order, no cash or C.O.D.s please.

Mr/Ms _____

Address _____

City/State _____ Zip _____

SVT3-12/92

Please allow four to six weeks for delivery.
Prices and availability subject to change without notice.